NEW PIECES FOR TRUMPET: BOOK II

GRADES 5 & 6

AB 1686

PAGEANT

Arthur Wills

4

SERENADE

Andrew Byrne

SCHERZO

12

NEW PIECES FOR TRUMPET: BOOK II

PAGEANT

Arthur Wills

SERENADE

Andrew Byrne

SCHERZO

Christopher Brown

POWER STATION

Andrew Byrne

FANFARE FOR ARIEL

Raymond Warren

MUSIC FOR PROSPERO

Raymond Warren

A.B. 1686

Processed and printed by
Halstan & Co. Ltd., Amersham, Bucks., England

The Associated Board's series of new
pieces for wind instruments covers Grades 3–6.
Two books are available for flute, oboe,
clarinet, bassoon, trumpet and horn:
and one book for trombone.

For a list of all the Board's publications,
please write to the Publications Department,
14 Bedford Square, London WC1B 3JG.

POWER STATION

Andrew Byrne

14

FANFARE FOR ARIEL

Raymond Warren

MUSIC FOR PROSPERO

Raymond Warren

22

A.B. 1686

N

24

Processed and printed by
Halstan & Co. Ltd., Amersham, Bucks., England